Soldier and Tsar in the Forest

A Russian tale translated by Richard Lourie

Pictures by URI SHULEVITZ

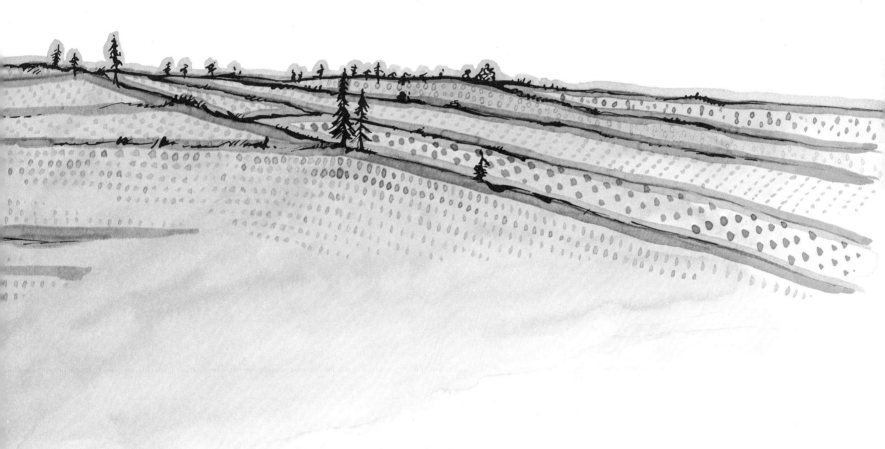

Farrar, Straus and Giroux / *New York*

To Michael di Capua
U.S.

Soldier and Tsar in the Forest is story 340 in
the three-volume Alexander Afanasyev collection of Russian tales

Pictures copyright © 1972 by Uri Shulevitz / Translation copyright © 1972 by Farrar, Straus and Giroux, Inc. /
All rights reserved / Library of Congress catalog card number: 72–188254 / ISBN 0–374–37126–1 / Published
simultaneously in Canada by Doubleday Canada Ltd., Toronto / Printed in the United States of America by Pearl
Pressman Liberty / Bound by A. Horowitz and Son / Typography by Jane Byers Bierhorst / First edition, 1972

Long ago and far away there lived a peasant who had two sons. The older son was taken to serve in the army of the tsar. He was a good and loyal soldier and, with the help of a little luck, he worked his way up to the rank of general. Soon after, an order for more soldiers went out and this time the younger son was taken. And it just so happened that he ended up in the very regiment commanded by his brother. The soldier was about to say hello to his brother, the general; but no, the general renounced him and said: "I don't know you, and don't pretend you know me."

One night the soldier was standing guard by the sentry box near the general's quarters. The general was giving a big banquet and many officers and rich lords were arriving. Seeing the happy guests and feeling how miserable he was, the soldier started to weep bitter tears. The guests questioned him: "Hey there, soldier, why are you crying?"

"Why shouldn't I cry? My very own brother is giving a party and having his fun, but he never gives me a second thought."

The guests asked the general about this and the general grew very angry: "And you believe him? He's lying through his teeth!" Then the general ordered that his brother be taken off the watch and that three hundred sticks be broken across his back, to make sure he would never again pretend to be part of the general's family.

The soldier's feelings were hurt as badly as his back and so he ran away from his regiment. Not very much later he came to a forest so wild and so dense that very few people had ever even peeked into it. But the forest suited him fine and he whiled away his time eating roots and berries.

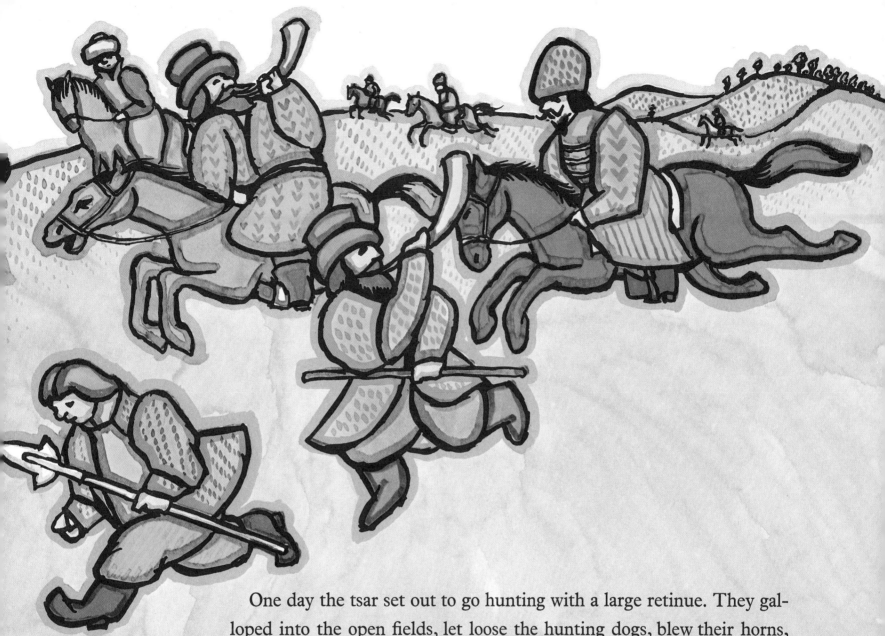

One day the tsar set out to go hunting with a large retinue. They gal-
loped into the open fields, let loose the hunting dogs, blew their horns,
and set to the fun of the hunt. Suddenly from out of nowhere jumped a
beautiful stag that flashed like an arrow past the tsar and leaped with a
splash into the river. It swam across to the other side and ran right into
the forest. The tsar chased after it on his horse, galloping and swimming,
swimming and galloping, but when he looked around, the stag was out
of sight. The hunting party had stayed far behind him and now he was
surrounded by the thick, dark forest.

Which way was out? He couldn't tell, there wasn't a single path to be seen. So he wandered till nightfall and grew very weary. Then who should he meet but the runaway soldier.

"Hello, good sir," said the soldier. "How did you find your way here?"

"By accident. I went out hunting and got lost in the forest. Lead me out to the road, will you, brother?"

"And who might you be?"

"A servant of the tsar."

"Well, it's dark now. We'd better spend the night somewhere down in the ravine. Then tomorrow I'll lead you out to the road."

So off they went to find a place to spend the night. They walked on and on and then they saw a peasant's house.

"Aha, God's sent us a night's lodging. Let's go in," said the soldier. They went into the house, where an old woman was sitting.

"Hello, granny," said the soldier.

"Hello, soldier."

"Give us something to eat and drink."

"I'd be eating right now if there were food in the house."

"You're lying, you old hag!" said the soldier and he started rummaging about in the stove and on the shelves. And sure enough, the old woman had lots of everything—there was wine aplenty and all kinds of food just ready to eat. They sat down at the table, ate to their heart's content, and then climbed up to the attic to sleep. The soldier said to the tsar: "God takes care of the careful. Let one of us rest and the other stand guard." They cast lots and the tsar had to stand guard.

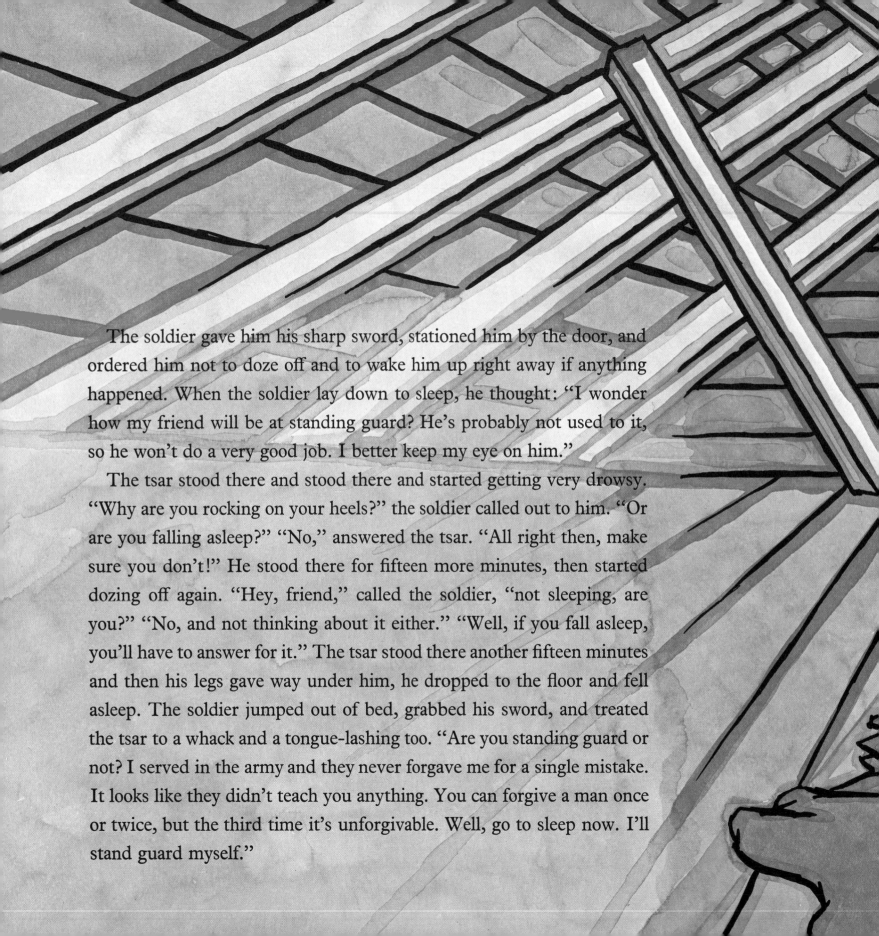

The soldier gave him his sharp sword, stationed him by the door, and ordered him not to doze off and to wake him up right away if anything happened. When the soldier lay down to sleep, he thought: "I wonder how my friend will be at standing guard? He's probably not used to it, so he won't do a very good job. I better keep my eye on him."

The tsar stood there and stood there and started getting very drowsy. "Why are you rocking on your heels?" the soldier called out to him. "Or are you falling asleep?" "No," answered the tsar. "All right then, make sure you don't!" He stood there for fifteen more minutes, then started dozing off again. "Hey, friend," called the soldier, "not sleeping, are you?" "No, and not thinking about it either." "Well, if you fall asleep, you'll have to answer for it." The tsar stood there another fifteen minutes and then his legs gave way under him, he dropped to the floor and fell asleep. The soldier jumped out of bed, grabbed his sword, and treated the tsar to a whack and a tongue-lashing too. "Are you standing guard or not? I served in the army and they never forgave me for a single mistake. It looks like they didn't teach you anything. You can forgive a man once or twice, but the third time it's unforgivable. Well, go to sleep now. I'll stand guard myself."

So the tsar lay down and the soldier stood guard, never blinking an eye.
Suddenly he heard men whistling and banging about—robbers had come
to the house. The old woman met them and said: "We have some guests
spending the night."

"That's good, granny. We've been hunting around for someone to rob
all night. Now it looks like we're in luck. But first give us some dinner
to eat."

"Our guests ate up everything. Drank everything up too."

"Aha, brave boys! And where are they now?"

"They went off upstairs to sleep."

"Good, I'll go make short work of them," said one of the robbers.

He took his big knife and climbed up to the attic. Just as he stuck his head through the door, *swoosh* went the soldier's sword and off rolled the robber's head. The soldier pulled the body into the attic, then stood waiting to see what would happen next. Downstairs, the robbers waited and waited, then one of them said: "What's keeping him so long?" So they sent another one up and the soldier killed him too. And in a little while he'd polished them all off.

The tsar woke up at dawn, saw all the dead robbers, and said: "What's been going on here?" The soldier told him everything that had happened. When they came down from the attic, the soldier caught sight of the old woman and shouted at her: "Stop, you old hag! I've got a score to settle with you. So your house is a robbers' den, is it! Well, now you give us all your money!" The old woman opened up a trunk full of gold. The soldier stuffed all his pockets with gold, then said to the tsar: "You take some too." But the tsar said: "No, brother, there's no need to. Our tsar has plenty of money already and what is his is ours." "You know best," said the soldier and led the tsar out of the forest up to a wide road.

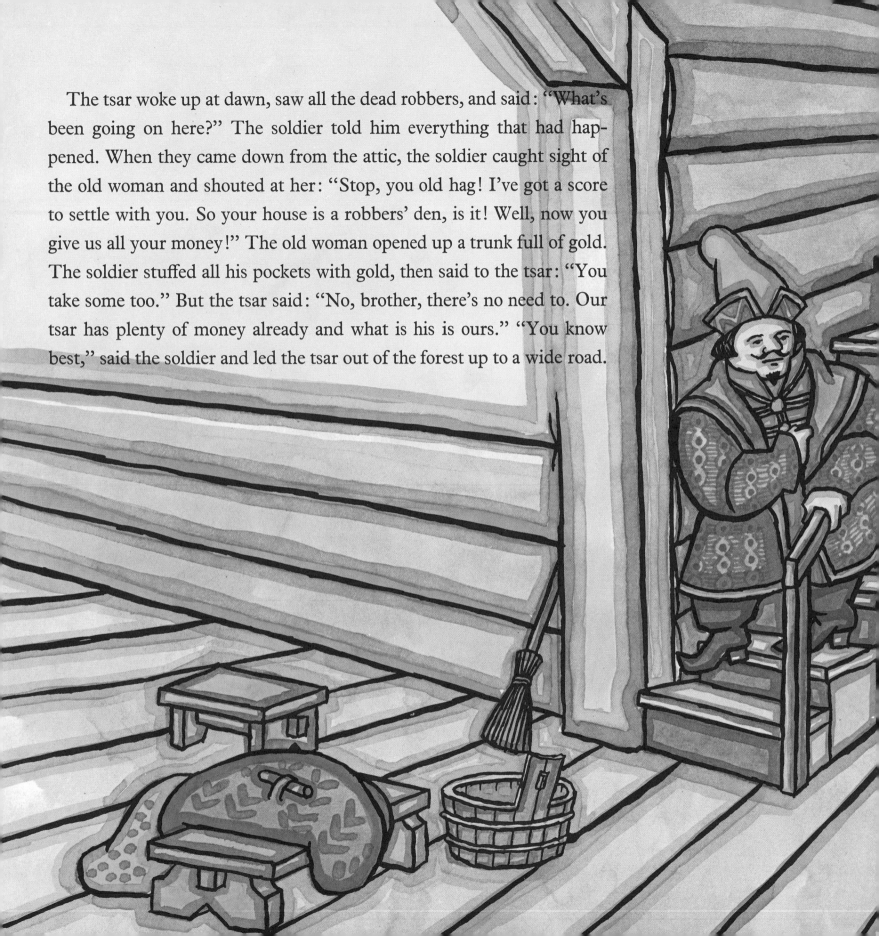

"Stick to this road," said the soldier, "and in an hour you'll be in the city."

"Farewell," said the tsar, "and thank you for your help. Come see me and I will make you a happy man."

"There's no use lying. I'm a runaway soldier. If I show my face in the city, they'll grab me in a minute."

"Take my word, soldier. The tsar loves me very much. If I intercede for you and tell him of your courage, he'll not only forgive you—he'll reward you as well."

"And how can I find you?"

"Just come right to the palace."

"All right then, I'll be there tomorrow."

The tsar said goodbye to the soldier and set out on the road. Just as soon as he arrived in the capital city, he gave orders to the soldiers at the gates, the guardhouses, and the sentry posts to be on the lookout for the soldier. The minute they saw him, they were to salute him like a general. The next day, when the soldier showed up in the city, all the sentries came running and saluted him. The soldier wondered: "What does all this mean?" and he asked: "Who are you saluting?" "You, soldier!" they answered. He took some gold pieces out of his pocket and gave them to the sentries to buy vodka. Wherever he walked in the city, the sentries saluted him—just try to figure out how much gold that cost him! "That servant of the tsar, what a chatterbox!" thought the soldier. "He's gone and told everyone how much money I've got."

So he went to the palace. The army was assembled there and the tsar came out to greet him wearing the same clothes he had worn for the hunt. It was only then that the soldier understood who had spent the night with him in the forest, and he grew very frightened. "It's the tsar! And I treated him like nobody special! I even gave him a whack with my sword!"

But the tsar took the soldier by the hand, thanked him for saving his life, made him a general, and reduced his brother to the ranks. Which just goes to show what happens when you renounce your very own brother, your own flesh and blood.